MORE *to read*

The Secret Hedgehog

Written and illustrated by
Paul Adshead

Child's Play (International) Limited
Swindon   New York

Dedicated to my family, but in particular to my mother,
who inspired a certain character in this story!
And, not forgetting Humphrey Pincushion, Pamela Prickle
and Little Horace, without whom this book
may not have been written.

Chapter 1

The Chicken and the Beaver

Mrs Carter takes our class for Science Studies.
She loves animals and knows heaps about them.

It was her idea, one Friday afternoon,
that we should all keep a Nature Notebook.

For everyone else in the class, it was
just another project. But for me
it was the start of a great adventure.

Of course, I didn't know that then . . .

Mrs Carter told us to start work straight away
by planning our project and drawing a picture.
We could study the wildlife in our gardens and
our pets as well, if we wanted.

But I was the only one
in the whole class
without a pet –
not even a goldfish!

And why was that?

Because my mother is
the FUSSIEST mother
in the world.

She says,

"Pets are MESSY.
Pets make WORK.
I want my house to be
PERFECTLY CLEAN and PERFECTLY TIDY."

1

In the Autumn, she made me sweep up the leaves
in the garden every afternoon and I was never
allowed to put out food for the birds.

One afternoon,
a seagull swooped down
and did a big Billy Bonga
on Mum's best dress.

She had a fit,
running round the garden,
waving her duster and
shouting at the top
of her voice what she would do to that seagull
if he ever came near her garden again.

So, you can imagine me sitting there,
that Friday afternoon in Science Studies,
with my head in my hands, thinking to myself,

"THIS IS GOING TO BE THE DULLEST
NATURE NOTEBOOK ON EARTH!"

It was as if Mrs Carter had heard, for she
looked at me and said,

"You can draw any animal you like."

I was always imagining people as animals,
so I picked up my pencil and drew Mum and Dad.

I drew Mum as a fussy little chicken,
clucking bossily about,
keeping her nest
neat and tidy.

I drew Dad
as a fat beaver,
with sticking-out
teeth, snoring
in the armchair!

During the day he *is* as busy as a beaver,
but you should see him in the evening.
He falls asleep by the fireside, with his shoes off.
It infuriates my mother.
She says he makes the whole room untidy.

When Mrs Carter saw my pictures, she said,

"Well, really, a chicken and a beaver!
You had better take this project seriously,
young man, or you'll be staying in after school!"

It was so unfair. There wasn't any wildlife
in our garden. I didn't have a pet.
Mrs Carter was cross with me, and it wasn't
my fault. I stared angrily at my Notebook,
then I drew a picture of a worm.
Mrs Carter said 'Good', and let me go home
when the bell went.

As I set off, I started to plan
what I would put in the Notebook . . .

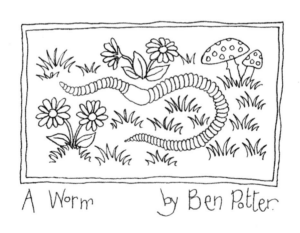

A Worm   by Ben Potter

Chapter 2

A Hedgehog Found

I went home past the pet shop, so that I could
write about the animals in the window.

There were a puppy, two kittens, a rabbit,
a parrot and a few mice. They were all asleep,
except for one mouse running in a wheel
and the parrot, which seemed to be doing
its best to wake up all the others!

Not much good for the Notebook.

I decided to walk home down the old lane
between Coppin Field and Long Meadow. I saw
some crows flapping about and two squirrels
chasing each other, but not much else.

I suppose I was making too much noise,
wading through the piles of leaves and
kicking them into the air.

All of a sudden, my foot hit something small and prickly. It flew up and then bounced, once, twice, three times, before rolling gently to a halt, a short way from where I stood.

At first, I thought it was one of those spiny seed cases that you find conkers in. I decided to find it and draw it in my Notebook.

But when I looked closely, I saw that it was a hedgehog. It was quite small, so I thought it must be a young one.

It looked weak and shivery. How could I leave it there to die? I decided there was only one thing to do. I had to take it home with me.

I wrapped it up in my scarf and tucked it
under my school jumper to keep it warm.
I felt like a kangaroo with a baby in my pouch!
I could feel it snuffling about as I sat
on the grass verge to make the first entry
in my Nature Notebook.

I would have to keep it a secret
from my mother and father.

My very first pet – A Secret Hedgehog!
My Nature Notebook would turn out
all right after all.

NATURE NOTEBOOK

ENTRY 1

Found young hedgehog by Coppin Field.

When I accidentally kicked it,
it flew up in the air,
curled up tight.

When it landed, it bounced
just like a ball.
That must be because of the spines.

When I looked at it closely,
I realised it was a young one,
because it was quite small
and a few of its spines
were still soft and pale.
Most of the spines
were hard and dark brown.

I must get a book from the library
as soon as I can, to find out
about the hedgehog and its spines.

I have seen several dead hedgehogs
on the road. They don't know
the highway code and drivers
don't seem to watch out for them.
So, many are run over!
They don't have any protection
from cars.

Chapter 3

A Village of Vultures

That afternoon, a terrible thing happened.

Before I went home, I had to get a box
for the hedgehog. The box had to be strong
and large enough for the little animal
to move around in, but small enough
to slide under my bed.

Thinking I might find one at The Corner Shop,
I turned and ran back to the village.

Nobody noticed me when I went into the shop.
It was busy and people were chatting
to each other by the till.
I picked up an empty box
and squeezed my way past the people.

Suddenly a voice hissed,

"And where do you think you are going?
Isn't there something you should be paying for?"

It was the lady behind the till.

I was puzzled. I thought people were allowed
to take boxes. But, as usual, I had forgotten
the strange way grown-ups' brains work.

I felt like a mouse cornered by an angry cat!

What a lot of fuss
about one tatty
old cardboard box!

I didn't notice that what the suspicious cat was staring at was the lump under the mouse's jumper! She wasn't talking about the box.

She glared over the rims of her glasses.

"I've a good mind to phone the police."

"I thought they were free," I said.
"Mum takes one or two every week."

That shocked her. She gazed at me with her mouth wide open and fanned herself with a packet of frozen fish fingers.

"So your mother is a shop-lifter too, is she?" she snapped.
"I think I should definitely phone the police."

I began to feel the cold grip of panic and,
worse still, a flock of hungry-looking vultures
had flown into the shop and crowded around me!

"That's Mrs Potter's boy!" exclaimed a vulture
with a large feather in her hat.
"Young rascal!"

"What are you hiding under your jumper?"
asked a fat vulture.

"I'll bet it's baked beans,"
laughed a vulture with a bald head.
"Are you running away from home, Sonny?"

My face was glowing red. I was angry and
lost for words. Slowly, it dawned on me that
it was not the box that was the cause of
all the trouble, but the lump under my jumper.
There was nothing for it but to tell my secret.

"It's a hedgehog."

"A likely story!"
exclaimed the lady behind the till.

They did not believe a word.

I took out the bundle from under my jumper,
unwrapped the scarf and revealed the tiny, sleepy
ball of prickles.

I didn't wait to see their faces, but shot
out of the door, clutching the hedgehog
in one hand and the box in the other.
So much for it being a SECRET hedgehog.
By the next afternoon, half the village
would know about it.

Still, at least I had the box!

NATURE NOTEBOOK
ENTRY 2

When I carried the hedgehog
under my jumper, he curled up,
which is what hedgehogs do
when they are frightened.
I will try to find out why and how.

Had great problems finding a box,
but got one in the end.
All I need now is some newspaper
and a hot water bottle.

Chapter 4

A Very Fussy Chicken

When I arrived home, the chicken (my mother)
was busy cooking in the kitchen,
so I was able to sneak the box up to my room
without being spotted.

I found a huge stack
of old comics under the bed,
tore them up and padded out
the box. The bedding was
all ready and I put
the hedgehog inside.

It opened its eyes and
peered over the edge
of its new home.
The box fitted snugly
under the bed.

As quiet as a mouse, I crept
into the bathroom, filled
a hot water bottle and wrapped
it in a towel. I tip-toed back
to my room without a sound.
I put the hot water bottle
into the hedgehog's box,
and slid the box
under the bed.

Just then, my mother called from downstairs.
"Dinner's on the table!"

I had to go. Guess what Mother asked, the very
minute I walked through the kitchen door?
"What have you been up to?"

She always knew when I was hiding something.

I tried to look sweet and innocent and said,
"Nothing, Mummy."

I thought it would fool her, but I should have
known better.

As I rushed through my dinner, I began
to wonder what hedgehogs eat.
I had a vague sort of feeling that they liked
bread and milk.

I waited until my mother went out of
the kitchen to say something to Dad. Then
I shoved a slice of bread into my pocket.
I picked up my mug of milk and crept upstairs
while the coast was clear.

Perhaps I shouldn't have been so quiet,
because when Mother found I had left the table,
she became suspicious and came upstairs to find me.

17

Her hawk-like eyes
scoured the room for evidence . . .

Her ears
seemed to quiver,
as they listened
for any unusual noises . . .

And she even sniffed
with her big bloodhound's nose.

But everything appeared
to be in order.

It looked as if the hedgehog was the ideal secret pet. He would sleep all day, while 'Mother Dear' was snooping about, and would wake only at night, when she and Dad were safely in bed.

I would have to watch out, though. She was bound to suspect something soon.

As she went back downstairs, she shouted,

"If I find out you've got an animal up there, you know what will happen!"

What did she think I was? Stupid? I knew exactly what would happen. A few weeks before, I had brought an injured seagull home and tried to feed it sardines on the kitchen table.

Mother had gone berserk, chasing the seagull round and round the kitchen. The seagull dropped Billy Bongas all over the place, before flying out through the back door. The whole room ponged of fish for ages!

NATURE NOTEBOOK

ENTRY·3

I put comics and
a hot water bottle
in the hedgehog's bed.
He should be warm enough.
I made sure that the bottle
was carefully wrapped in a towel,
so that he wouldn't burn himself.

I am not sure what hedgehogs eat,
but I have given him
some bread and milk.

I do hope hedgehogs are not
as messy as seagulls!

Chapter 5

Mrs Carter and Mitzi to the Rescue

I sat in my room, bursting to tell my secret to someone. But who could I tell? I also needed a few tips on hedgehog care.

That was when I thought of Mrs Carter. She lived quite near and I could show her all the things I was doing for my Notebook. She was sure to be impressed.

I ran downstairs and asked my mother if I could go to see Mrs Carter and ask her about my homework. She told me to be sure I was home by seven.

I took the long way round and stopped at the library on the way. It was open until six o'clock on Fridays. I got there just in time, found a good book about hedgehogs, then hurried on to Mrs Carter's.

When she opened the door, her puppy, Mitzi, came bounding to greet me. (Fancy calling a dog MITZI! My dog will be called Scamp or Bouncer. At least, it will if I ever have one).

I played with Mitzi for a bit and almost forgot to ask about the hedgehog!

I told Mrs Carter my hedgehog was too young to look after himself and I had rescued him and given him a bed and some bread and milk.

Well, when I said bread and milk, her eyes
nearly popped out of her head.

"You mustn't feed a hedgehog on bread and
milk!" she exclaimed. "Milk will make it ill!"

"You can give it some dog food. Mitzi has
a few spare tins. I'll give you one."

She warned me that wild animals were not meant
to be kept as pets and that it would not be
an easy task to look after one.

I rushed home as fast as a cheetah.
I had to get to that saucer of bread
and milk before he did. It was a matter
of life and death!

I got home, panting, and dashed
into my bedroom. Carefully, I pulled
the box out from under the bed.

I let out a sigh of relief. The hedgehog was
fast asleep. He hadn't touched the bread and
milk. I took the saucer out of the box and put
it beside my bed.

Hedgehogs do not eat bread and milk.

There is something in milk, called lactose, which they cannot digest and which makes them too weak to fight against germs that attack them.

They can even die.

In the wild, hedgehogs eat quite a lot of different things, including slugs, beetles, caterpillars and earthworms. They even scavenge dead frogs and young mice or voles.

Dad must like hedgehogs for eating some of the pests. I bet all gardeners like them! And farmers, too.

Good! Mrs Carter

Hedgehogs have a very tight skin muscle which works like an elastic band or draw-string to keep them curled up tight, with their arms, legs and snout tucked inside. It looks like a good way for them to protect themselves.

Very few animals can harm hedgehogs, because of their spines, except for badgers. Badgers have very long claws, even longer than the spines of the hedgehog, and they can use them to kill and uncurl their prey.

Chapter 6

Strong Medicine

Just at that moment, I heard footsteps.
They were coming closer and, by the sound
of them, they could only be my mother's.
I just had time to slide the box under the bed,
before the bedroom door burst open and
she stalked in like a hungry tiger.

She said she was worried in case I felt ill,
since I had rushed straight up to my room
without saying good night or eating any supper.
(More likely, she was just being nosy!).

I sat on the bed feeling rather smug.
The hedgehog was well hidden,
and so was my notebook.

But guess what? I had forgotten the saucer
of bread and milk on the bedside table.
I tried to stand in front of it, but, as usual,
old Hawk Eyes spotted it and asked,
"What on earth is that?"

For a moment, my mind went blank as I searched
for an excuse. Then suddenly I had an idea.

"It's my supper," I explained.

"Your supper!" She gasped. "It looks awful."
(That was true!)

"Then why aren't you eating it?"

"Er .. I forgot to bring a spoon," I tried.

I suggested going downstairs to eat
in the kitchen. I had an awful feeling
I was getting myself into deeper trouble.
Like a fly, the more I struggled,
the worse I got tangled in the web.

Imagine my dismay when the spider herself
handed me a spoon out of her apron pocket!
It was just like her to be wearing an apron
at that time of night.

Come to think of it, I've never seen her
without an apron on. I wonder if she goes
to bed in it, over the top of her nightie!

She told me to sit on the bed and eat it all up.
I said I wasn't hungry. That convinced her
I was ill. She felt my forehead, looked at my
tongue and was just about to get a thermometer,
when something moved by the door.

I could not believe my eyes. A small prickly
object was making its way out of the door
and along the landing. If Mother turned round,
she was bound to see it.

"I feel fine," I shouted heartily.

I tried to prove it by shovelling large spoonfuls
of sloppy bread and milk into my mouth,
while wearing my most contented smile.

It worked. But better still, it gave the hedgehog
a chance to crawl into the bathroom.
And that gave me a brilliant idea.

"I'm going to be sick," I gasped,
half wondering if I really was.

I rushed into the bathroom, locked the door,
and flushed the bread and milk down the loo.
While it was making its flushing noises,
I shut the hedgehog in the bathroom cupboard
with the shampoo and bath salts!

Mum was yelling like mad to be let in,
so I opened the door and staggered out
with a towel over my mouth. I tried hard
to look pale and sickly, but the towel
hid an enormous grin.

I had managed to get rid of that yukky food AND
hide the hedgehog for the time being.

I let my mother help me undress and
got into bed.

Then to finish off my day, she gave me
two enormous spoonfuls of the most revolting
medicine in the world!

NATURE NOTEBOOK

ENTRY 5

The hedgehog crawled from my bedroom
to the bathroom. I noticed he made
a few wet drips on the way.
They had come from his nose.
This seems to happen when hedgehogs
are on to an interesting scent.

They have a very powerful sense
of smell. Their noses are very sensitive,
which is why they are kept so moist.
Dogs have moist noses, too.

Very observant! Mrs C.

Hedgehogs live for about six years.
But not many survive that long.
Some die because of bad weather,
or from not finding enough food,
or having an accident.

Chapter 7
Silver-back Gorilla to the Rescue

I woke up suddenly. It was pitch black and I could hear mysterious noises like someone prowling about.

It's a burglar! I thought.

I checked the time on my clock. The hands shone brightly in the dark. They pointed to two o'clock.

I heard the noise again, bumping and crashing, like someone knocking things over in the bathroom.

He was a pretty clumsy burglar.
Come to think of it, what was there to steal in the bathroom anyway? Nothing we would miss.

I would have to go and investigate.
I took my cricket bat, and decided to catch him unawares, whack him over the head and tie him up in the shower curtain.

I could just imagine the headlines in the daily paper:

BOY CATCHES BURGLAR SINGLE-HANDED!

I might even have to go on telly.

I imagined I was a gigantic silver-back gorilla, protecting my territory from hunters . . .

The giant silver-back gorilla crept through the tropical undergrowth along the landing.
With a blood-curdling yell, he leapt into the bathroom, turned on the light, and brandished his cricket bat.

To his surprise the bathroom was empty.
He was just thinking about going back to bed,
when the most feared and deadly creature
in the entire rainforest appeared –
the gigantic silver-back gorilla's Mother!

Mother rushed out onto the landing in a state
of complete panic. (Dad snored through
the whole thing – I think he could sleep
through a thunderstorm!)

The sight of my mother with her hair spiked up
in rollers, reminded me of something.
She didn't look like a gorilla. She didn't
look like a tiger or even a chicken.

She looked exactly like a HEDGEHOG!!!

Everything fell into place.
I had completely forgotten
the secret hedgehog,
which was wide awake
and looking for a way out of the cupboard.

"What's all this noise about?"
gasped my mother.

I was about to say the usual 'Oh, nothing',
when I realised that she was never going
to believe I was rushing about
with a cricket bat in the middle of the night
and yelling, simply for nothing.

So I told her there was a burglar.

"You poor thing, you're delirious," she said.
"I knew you were sickening for something.
You'd better not go to school tomorrow."

I wasn't going to argue with that.
I let her take me back to bed and tuck me in.
I just hoped that the hedgehog wouldn't knock
anything else over before she was asleep again
in her own bed.

As soon as it was safe, I crept like a shadow
to the bathroom cupboard and sneaked
the hedgehog back in my dressing gown pocket.

I put him under the bed and he gobbled up
the saucer of mashed up dog food. He was
a very noisy eater and made yukky slurping
noises, just like my father when he eats soup.

For the rest of the night, I let him roam
around the room. I thought he could do
with the exercise.

I set my alarm for seven-thirty, so I could get
the hedgehog back in his box before Mother came
in to open my curtains in the morning.

I fell asleep exhausted! Surely nothing else
could go wrong, could it?

NATURE NOTEBOOK
ENTRY 6

Gave the hedgehog some dog food.
He loved it. Then I did
some homework on young hedgehogs.

Hedgehogs are born head-first
and on their backs.
They weigh about 12–25 grams
and are about 5.5 cm long.

By 11 days old, they can curl up.
Soon after, their eyes and ears
open and they start to grow hair
on their face and tummy.
At about three weeks old
their teeth start to come through.

When the babies are hungry,
they give a high-pitched squeak.
Their mother suckles them until
they are about 42–44 days old.
By 6–8 weeks, all the parts
of their body are developed,
but they are still very small.

50% do not survive their first winter.

Chapter 8

Oh, No! The Hedgehog Has Gone!

I woke up to the sound of my alarm clock.
I leapt out of bed and started to get ready
for school. Then I remembered Mum saying
I could have the day off. And then I realised
it was Saturday. I didn't have to go, anyway.

I had forgotten the hedgehog. I had to find
him quickly, before Mum came in.

I spent twenty minutes searching my room, but
only found a few rather smelly hedgehog droppings.

He had to be in there somewhere,
as the door had been shut all night.

I told myself to keep calm and try to imagine
where I would go if I were a hedgehog.

It was fun, but it didn't help much.
I imagined crawling into Mum and Dad's room and
curling up in one of Mother's slippers.

I can just picture the look of horror
on her face as she hopped round the room,
after pricking her toes!

At that moment I heard a muffled, scuffling
noise from behind the cupboard. Surely,
he couldn't have squeezed behind there!
I went to investigate!

He had!!!

I tried to move the cupboard, but it was far too heavy.

I piled all my clothes on the bed, but it was
still too heavy. I pulled all my toys out,
then my shoes and finally an enormous pile of
books and jigsaws.

I felt like an overworked donkey.

The bed was piled high with odds and ends
and my room looked like an explosion in a junkyard!
Anyway, when the cupboard was completely empty,
it was just light enough for me to shift slightly.

Eeek . . .!

As I peered behind the cupboard, I had
the fright of my life. For there stood
a small, fluffy, grey, rat-like creature.
It turned slowly towards me. I yelled
with surprise. But something about
its shuffling walk and black shiny nose looked
familiar. It WAS the hedgehog after all.

The cupboard had not been moved for ages.
There was masses of dust and grey fluff.
The hedgehog must have squeezed its way along,
like a little walking brush, and gathered
all that fluff on his spines.

I picked him up. I think he knew who I was
by now, because he didn't curl up. I didn't
know whether I should take him to the bathroom
and rinse him under the taps. But then,
to my horror, I heard the dreaded footsteps . . .

NATURE NOTEBOOK

ENTRY 7

At around 9–11 months, hedgehogs are old enough to mate. They start breeding in April and it takes five to six weeks before the young hedgehogs are born.

From what I've seen, it looks as though hedgehogs spend most of the day asleep and most of the night awake.

Yes, we call that being 'nocturnal'.

Mrs C.

Chapter 9

Spring Cleaning

The handle on my door started to turn . . . . Mother
was coming in. Quickly, I slipped the hedgehog
back in his box.
"What have you been doing?"

That was a hard one to answer, but once again
I had one of my brilliant ideas and said,

"I'm trying to push the cupboard back.
I was cleaning behind it. I don't think
it has been done for ages!"

She looked at me in amazement. Watching me eat
a saucer of bread and milk had seemed strange.
Then to wake up in the middle of the night
to find me attacking an imaginary burglar was
stranger still. Now she had found me spring-cleaning
my bedroom first thing in the morning.
That must have been the strangest thing of all.

By lunch time I was fed up. I had wasted
the whole morning tidying my room.

On any other Saturday, I would be out
on my bike. But since I had started, my mother
insisted that we spring clean the whole room.
She had made sure that everything was clean and
neat and exactly where it belonged.

She said it should have been done months ago. As she walked out of the bedroom she moaned about all the rubbish she had taken downstairs.

She told me that she had found an old box of torn-up comics under the bed and had taken it downstairs with all the other rubbish!

I could hardly believe my ears. Imagine, if she had known there was a hedgehog in the box!

So there I was, wondering if I could sneak downstairs and get the hedgehog back without my mother noticing. But she had already told me to stay in my room, and that I was not well enough to eat any lunch.

Thanks a lot, Mum!!! How come I was well enough to spend the entire morning tidying my room?

Just then the doorbell rang.

Would I ever be able to save the hedgehog?

NATURE NOTEBOOK

ENTRY 8

I am very interested
in the hedgehog's spines.
They help him bounce and protect
him from other animals and people,
but how do hedgehogs get them?

Hedgehogs are born with about 100
soft white spines which are covered
by a thin layer of skin. As soon as
hedgehogs are born, the spines start
to come through the skin.
Within two days, a set of darker spines
starts growing through. After 7 days,
there is a full set of brown spines.

By 6–8 weeks, hedgehogs have
a full set of adult spines
which last 2–3 years and
are gradually replaced, one by one.

A large adult may have 6,000–7,000 spines.

Chapter 10

The Camel's Visit

My mother called up the stairs to tell me
that Doctor Merry was there to see me.
That was all I needed.

At least, I didn't have to pretend to be ill.
I was almost sick with worry. My only hope
was that the hedgehog would stay asleep,
until I had a chance to rescue it.

But this was no ordinary hedgehog. He did not
stay asleep. And what is more, feeling
rather annoyed at being disturbed by Mother,
he climbed out of the box. It must have happened
while Doctor Merry was examining me.

Doctor Merry was a tall, thin gentleman,
with a permanently gloomy expression
and a bedside manner to match. He always
reminded me of an extremely depressed camel!

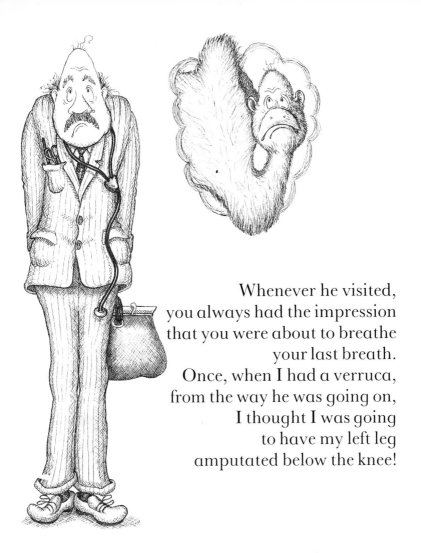

Whenever he visited,
you always had the impression
that you were about to breathe
your last breath.
Once, when I had a verruca,
from the way he was going on,
I thought I was going
to have my left leg
amputated below the knee!

On this visit, it was almost as bad. He poked
and prodded me everywhere. With a great deal
of tut-tutting and shaking of his head,
he announced in his gloomiest voice that
he could find nothing wrong with me whatsoever.

It was amazing, after all the strain I'd been under.

Anyway, as soon as he stepped into the bathroom to wash his hands, I asked my mother if I could go downstairs and have something to eat at last. She agreed. I dressed quickly and made my way downstairs, with the doctor a few paces behind, and Mother bringing up the rear.

As I led the way down, I saw to my great horror that the hedgehog was sitting right in the middle of the hall.

This would have been bad enough, but to make matters worse, he was chewing on the mat and spitting all over himself. He was already covered from head to claw in saliva.

Time stood still as I took in the full seriousness of the situation. If the Doctor saw the hedgehog, he would probably think I was about to come down with a severe attack of rabies and send me off to the isolation ward at the local hospital.

Worse still, if my Mother saw him, I would probably never be allowed out again in my whole life!

Something had to be done before anyone else saw the hedgehog. But what?

An idea flashed through my mind. Like a frog pouncing on a stray snail, I dived down the remaining stairs, pretending I was falling. As I hurtled towards the floor, I made a desperate grab at a hat that was hanging on the end of the bannister, slapped it over the hedgehog and pushed him under the hall table.

Seeing me fall, Doctor Merry suddenly brightened up. He might have a patient on his hands after all. He peered at me and asked if I was hurt anywhere. I scrambled to my feet and replied that I was fine.

While Mother showed Doctor Merry out, I retrieved the hedgehog and examined him. Was he ill, I wondered? No, he appeared perfectly happy and healthy. I slid him under my jumper and collapsed on the floor in a fit of hysterical laughter.

I was still gasping for breath when Mum walked back into the hall with the doctor still by her side. Trying desperately to keep my face straight, I stood up and asked if anything was wrong.

"Yes," replied Doctor Merry gloomily. "I seem to have forgotten my hat!"

NATURE NOTEBOOK
ENTRY 9

I was most puzzled to find
the hedgehog chewing the mat.
But now I understand.
Mrs Carter explained to me
a strange habit of hedgehogs.
They chew or lick an object
with an interesting smell
until they begin to foam
at the mouth.
Then the hedgehog turns
its head round over its back,
flicking the foam out
over its spines.

It could be that they want
to hide their own smell,
or maybe it's like an antiseptic
to keep them clean.
I'm not sure about that.

I'm not sure why they do this either,
but you have made two good guesses!

Mrs C.

49

Chapter 11

A Secret Shared

Well, it was obvious by now that the hedgehog was quite strong and lively. So, as I was having so much trouble keeping him a secret inside the house, I decided to find somewhere else to keep him, preferably outside!

I also made another important decision: to share the secret with my father.

He is good at keeping secrets. He keeps them all in his garden shed, which is always locked. Inside, he has a big comfy armchair, a primus stove, a kettle, a teapot, a couple of mugs, a big tin of biscuits and an enormous stack of adventure story books.

Whenever Mother scolds him too much, he says he is going to re-pot some seedlings or prune the roses, or perform another equally important task. Then he locks himself in the shed, makes a big pot of tea, and settles himself down for a few hours, peaceful reading.

Mother never tries to come into the shed. Dad is always telling her about the gigantic spiders there and cobwebs as big as dinner plates.

Mother is absolutely terrified of spiders.

That evening, straight after supper, Dad went down to the shed, saying he had to oil his hedge-clippers.

A few minutes later, I followed him down
and made our secret knock on the door,
so he would know it was only me. Then we sat
together in the armchair scoffing chocolate biscuits,
making as many crumbs as we wanted.

I told him the whole story. He laughed from
beginning to end. He has a really funny laugh.
He grunts and squeals like an excited pig,
which always gets me laughing as well.

By the time I had finished, we had tears
in our eyes. Finally, Dad managed to wheeze,
"Let's keep the little fellow in here,"
which was just what I had hoped he would say.

Dad gave me the spare key, so that later on,
when everyone was asleep,
I could take the hedgehog his food and
hot water bottle.

While Dad kept Mother talking, I sneaked upstairs, collected the box with the hedgehog in it, and carried it to the garden shed.

Usually, Mother and Father go to bed straight after the "News at Ten" on TV. Unfortunately, there was a documentary about "How the Vacuum Cleaner was invented", and Mother said she simply couldn't miss it.

As the seconds ticked by, I imagined my hungry little hedgehog climbing out of his box and exploring the shed. At last, the programme finished, but by now Mother was inspired to vacuum the whole sitting room before going to bed.

By the time she was safely asleep and I had got my torch, hot water bottle and saucer of dog food, it was well after midnight.

I quickly unlocked the shed door, hurried inside and shone my torch around. As I expected, the box was empty, but, to my great dismay, there was no sign of the hedgehog anywhere.

I searched and searched until I eventually found a small hole at the back of the shed, and, yes, there were a couple of hedgehog spines stuck into the wood.

The hedgehog had escaped!

I rushed out of the shed. In the light of
my torch I could see a line of little paw
prints in the damp soil, leading towards
the vegetable plot.

Between the shed and the plot lay the pond,
but instead of going round it, the footprints
led straight to the edge and stopped.
The hedgehog must have gone for a drink and
slipped in.

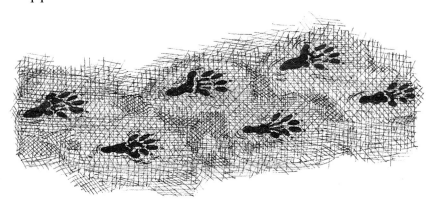

From the splashing sounds I could hear,
he was clearly still swimming around.

As I watched in the light of my torch,
wondering what to do, he swam to the edge and
climbed out.

He was soaked and the water was freezing.
He had survived the pond, but I decided
to take him back into the house,
to make sure he didn't catch a cold or
pneumonia, or something.

I didn't want him to end up being ill, after
going to so much trouble to rescue him.

Once again, I slid the box under my bed.
It took ages to get to sleep and, even when I
did, I kept having the most peculiar dreams.

When I finally awoke the following morning,
I had reached a very important decision.

NATURE NOTEBOOK
ENTRY 10

Hedgehog had a disaster last night.
He fell into the pond.
But it's only a small pond
and even though hedgehogs
are short-sighted,
he managed to swim to the edge
and climb out.

So, hedgehogs can swim.
Luckily, he could climb onto the rockery.
If it had been one of those
smooth-sided plastic ponds,
he would have been unable to climb out
and would have drowned.

That started me wondering
why there aren't any hedgehogs
in America or Australia?

Hedgehogs can be found all over Europe,
in New Zealand and in parts of North Russia.

There are also some other types
of hedgehogs (distant relations, I suppose),
who live in Africa and Asia.

Chapter 12

Good-bye Hedgehog

Well that was it, Nature Notebook or not,
it was going to be 'Good-bye, hedgehog',
as soon as it was dark.
In little more than a week-end,
he had caused me more problems than
anything else in my entire life. I only wanted
to help him, but that last escapade convinced me
that he wanted his freedom.

Anyway, that night, once Mum and Dad were
safely in bed again, I would give him one more
meal and send him on his way.

He didn't catch a cold. In fact, he was as fit
as a flea. And talking of fleas, if I didn't
get rid of him soon I would have enough
fleas to open my own performing flea circus!

When Mum and Dad were asleep,
I crept downstairs
with the hedgehog and took him
into the back garden,
where I waved him good-bye.

I was sorry to see him go,
but only a bit. He had eaten
well and had warmth and comfort.
So, as I climbed into bed,
I had no guilty feelings
about sending him on his way.

Two hours later I was still awake. I could not sleep for worry. It was a frosty night. I hoped the hedgehog would find somewhere nice and warm to sleep. He had had a good meal of dog food, so I had no reason to feel guilty.

The clock ticked loudly, the minutes passed, and still I could not sleep. I was really worried.

I sat up in bed with my torch and read about hedgehogs in my encyclopaedia.

I told myself not to feel guilty – there was no reason to.

NATURE NOTEBOOK
ENTRY 11

I let the hedgehog go free,
but I am worried
about him.

When there is a cold season,
like winter in England,
hedgehogs hibernate. This means
they curl up and look as though
they are in a deep sleep.

Sometimes they hibernate
in bonfires and get burned,
or they fall into plastic garden ponds
and drown.

Some get stuck in cattle grids and starve,
others get killed by cars,
or poisoned by slug pellet poison.

I have just sent my hedgehog to its doom.

Well done Ben. This is an excellent nature notebook.
Try not to worry about the hedgehog,
perhaps he is hibernating.
Mrs C.

Chapter 13

Life after Hedgehog

The next day, after lunch, Mrs Carter brought Mitzi round and said I could take her for a walk.

I found a squashed hedgehog by the edge
of the lane. I was sure it was mine.
I thought he had been knocked over by a car.

I scraped a hole in the ground with my hands
and buried him under a huge mound of leaves.
I stood for a full minute in silence and
thought about my prickly friend.

It was a very sad and solemn moment, except when Mitzi went and tiddled on the grave. (Just like a dog – no sense of occasion). I was never ever going to have another pet as long as I lived.

In the afternoon, Mrs Carter had a word with my parents about how much I loved animals. My Mother said I could have a goldfish, as long as I cleaned out its bowl each week.

First thing next morning, Dad took me straight round to the pet shop to buy one. We thought about getting a white rat and keeping it secretly in the garden shed. But to tell the truth, I've had quite enough of secrets for the time being!

Epilogue

I don't know what epilogue means, but there is often one at the end of a book.

I think it is when the author has finished the story, but then thinks of another bit he wants to add on.

I got a special commendation for my Nature Notebook. Mrs Carter said that everyone could learn a lot from my attempt to rescue a wild animal. She asked me to read it out aloud to the whole class.

To make it really interesting, I told them all the adventures I had had trying to keep it a secret, which the class thought was really funny.

Claire Shepherd (good in English) said it would make a really good book. She should know. Her mum used to work as a part-time cleaner for the first cousins of an assistant sub-editor's secretary at a publishers somewhere in Swindon.

It is now Spring. Last week, my mother and I were out in the garden when a hedgehog appeared at the end of the lawn.

I was so excited. I rushed down the path towards it and knelt gently by its side. To my delight, it didn't curl up in a tight prickly ball, like most hedgehogs would have done, but gazed up at me with a friendly snuffle.

I had no doubts at all. It was my SECRET HEDGEHOG! He must have gone into hibernation that frosty night when I let him go, and was hidden here in the garden all the time.

Mum bellowed out,

"Don't touch it, you don't know where it's been."

That made me laugh. I knew exactly where
he had been. But it was a good job
she never found out.

"That's our secret, isn't it?" I whispered
to the little creature beside me.

The secret hedgehog said nothing at all.
But from the twinkle in his eyes I was sure
he had understood every single word.

The End

Alexandra stella
Horvath